Stella
AND THE
Berry Thief

Stella
AND THE
Berry Thief

Jane B. Mason
ILLUSTRATED BY Loek Koopmans

Marshall Cavendish

NEW YORK LONDON SINGAPORE

Stella lived at the edge of a winding river, all by herself, which was just how she liked it. She did not have many friends or visit with her neighbors.

Most of Stella's time was spent in her garden tending flowers and vegetables—and raspberries.

Stella adored her raspberries. She grew bushes that were six feet tall, and every July they hung thick with the sweetest, juiciest berries in the whole state of Wisconsin. Stella's pies and preserves always won blue ribbons at the state fair.

"I don't know how such a sour woman can make such sweet preserves," Stella's neighbor, Serena Swenson, remarked to her husband as Stella tucked another blue ribbon into her market basket. "She never shares a single jar."

It was true. Aside from the one jar and one pie she brought to the fair each summer, Stella hoarded her preserves and pies as a squirrel hoards nuts. And all winter long she started each day in front of her kitchen fire with a mug of steaming tea and a slice of homemade bread slathered with her divine raspberry jam.

Then one summer, at the peak of berry season, something terrible happened.

Stella stepped out onto her front porch with her picking pail, as she did every Wednesday and Sunday in July. But when she reached the garden gate, her face scrunched into a terrible scowl. There was not a single red raspberry in sight.

"Some varmint has been stealing my berries!" Stella bellowed.

That winter Stella had only enough preserves to make
it through January. And as she drank her tea and ate
her bread with plain butter on a cold February morning,
she vowed that she would catch the scoundrel who had stolen
her berries.

That spring Stella gave her berry bushes plenty
of fertilizer and water and did extra weeding. And
in July, when the bushes were full of fruit, she had
a stakeout. Stella kept watch all night long from her
porch, her flashlight close at hand. The only trouble
was she kept dozing off. She tried reading. She tried
pinching herself. She could not stay awake. Finally, her
quiet snores filled the air.

The next morning, Stella sprang to her feet. She raced
out to her garden. The gate was open, and nearly every
ripe berry was gone!

Stella had to find out who was stealing her berries.
So she set a trap. Using an old bucket, some strong
twine, and a heap of compost, she fixed her garden
gate so that anyone who opened it would make a lot
of racket—and get a surprise.

That night Stella made a cozy bed for herself on her porch. She was dreaming about a big slice of berry pie when—crash!—she woke with a start. She quickly turned on her flashlight . . . and blinked. A black bear stood at her garden gate, covered in rotting vegetables.

The two stared at each other for several long moments. Then the bear gave the air a good long sniff and ambled back into the woods.

Stella kept the bucket of compost over her garden gate for a whole week and her eyes peeled for that bear.

Soon Stella's berry bushes hung thick with juicy fruit—enough for a good batch of preserves. She picked her way down the first row, and was starting on the second when she heard a growl near the gate. Peering through a berry bush, she saw the bear amble down another row, sit its big rump down, and begin its morning snack.

As quietly as she could, Stella tried to sneak away. But as soon as she took a step, the bear lifted its head to listen. Stella froze. She was trapped in her very own berry patch!

"Stupid bear," she grumbled. But she didn't say it very loud.

For the next several weeks, Stella tried everything
she could think of to keep the bear away from her berries.
She set up spotlights and left them on all night, but they
just helped him to see the berries better. She played her radio
really loud, but the bear seemed to enjoy the beat. Finally,
she sprayed the berries with hot sauce. This sent both of
them dashing for a drink.

Stella was miserable. At this rate, she'd barely have enough jam to get through November!

So the next time the bear came back, she tried something completely different: she kept on picking—at first very quietly—in her berry patch. After awhile she and the bear seemed to have a kind of understanding. And soon Stella and the bear found themselves picking in the same row.

"Those are my berries, you know," Stella blurted out as she watched the bear stuff a pawful into its mouth. The bear looked at Stella, sizing her up. Then it went back to picking berries.

"You're stealing them," Stella went on. "That makes you a common thief, just like that no-good brother-in-law of mine, Bernie. Maybe that's what I should call you—Bernie."

The bear let out a giant yawn, which Stella took as a sign.

"Bernie it is then," she declared. And for the first time since January, she felt a little bit satisfied.

But by now berry season was almost over, and Stella did not have enough berries for even a single batch of preserves. She was just coming out of her garden with a nearly empty pail when Bernie ambled up for his snack.

"The bushes are picked clean," Stella told him.

Bernie poked his nose through the garden gate and took a good whiff.

Then he started off into the forest.
When he reached the edge he gave a little
snort and looked back at Stella.

Stella paused for one tiny second. Then, keeping a respectful distance, she followed him. First Bernie turned over several rotting logs and ate some grubs and slugs. Then he had a good back scratch on a tall pine tree. Finally Bernie led Stella across a large field . . .

. . . where he sat down in front of the biggest raspberry patch Stella had ever seen.

Stella rushed forward, plucked a berry off the bramble, and popped it into her mouth. It was delicious—full of flavor and sweetness. "Ambrosia!" she declared. And she got right to work.

Stella spent the whole day picking berries. She picked and picked and picked, long after Bernie had eaten his fill and wandered away.

Then she hurried home and made a half dozen pies and three large batches of preserves. She was up until two o'clock in the morning rolling out crusts, simmering her berries, and adding just the right amount of sweeteners, seasonings, and pectin.

The next day, Stella got up at the crack of dawn and drove to the fair. She proudly laid a pie and preserves on the table, as the judges made their way up and down the aisles sampling each offering.

Miss Appleberry dribbled a glob of raspberry jam on her chin.

"Absolutely delicious," Mr. Silver said as he smacked his lips over the last of a slice of pie.

The judges agreed. Stella's pie and preserves won blue ribbons, "best of the fair."

Stella beamed. And for the rest of the afternoon she did something she had never done before—she shared her pies and preserves with folks at the fair. She even sent her neighbor, Serena Swenson, home with two jars of preserves. And that night she left a pie next to her garden gate for her good friend, Bernie.

Text copyright © 2004 by Jane B. Mason
Illustrations copyright © 2004 by Loek Koopmans
All rights reserved.
Marshall Cavendish
99 White Plains Road, Tarrytown, NY 10591
www.marshallcavendish.com

Library of Congress Cataloging-in-Publication Data

Mason, Jane B.
Stella and the berry thief / by Jane B. Mason;
illustrations by Loek Koopmans.-- 1st ed.
p. cm.
Summary: Stella, who never shares her ribbon-winning raspberry pies and
preserves with anyone, wonders what to do about a bear that starts
stealing her berries.
ISBN 0-7614-5123-4
[1. Raspberries--Fiction. 2. Bears--Fiction.]   I. Koopmans, Loek, ill.
II. Title.
PZ7.M4116St 2004
[E]--dc21   2003009317

The text of this book is set in 16-point Colwell Roman.
The illustrations are rendered in watercolor.
Book design by E. Friedman

Printed in China
FIRST EDITION
1 2 4 6 5 3